I0570680

Dark Parchments

MIDNIGHT
CURSES & VERSES

By MICHAEL H. HANSON

MoonDream
PRESS

An Imprint of Copper Dog Publishing, LLC

Dark Parchments

Copyright ©2015 Copper Dog Publishing, LLC

Published by Moondream Press, an imprint of Copper Dog Publishing, LLC
537 Leader Circle
Louisville, CO 80027

Visit our Web site: www.copperdogpublishing.com

Credits:
Cover and Interior Design: Helen Harrison

Dark Parchments written by Michael H. Hanson

Cover art: Let Them Eat Cake,
Copyright ©Chris Mars/Chris Mars Publishing, Inc.
www.chrismarspublishing.com

Library of Congress Control Number: 2015917133

ISBN: 978-1-943690-03-9 Print

ISBN: 978-1-943690-04-6 ePub

First Edition: October 2015

All Poems Copyright ©2015 Moondream Press, an imprint of Copper Dog Publishing, LLC

"All Hallow's Eve" and "Anna-Lee" – originally published in Autumn Blush, ©2007 Racket River Press.

"Awaken", "Gehenna Dreams", "In The Trees", "Shadow Puppets", & "Cartoon Hitman" – originally published in Jubilant Whispers, ©2010 Racket River Press.

Printed in the United States of America

Table of Contents

FOREWORD 7

The Poems

GEHENNA DREAMS 13

DOPPELGÄNGER 14

THE FIRST WAVE 15

REMEMBRANCE 16

HALLOWEENLAND 17

SHE'S SUFFOCATING 18

FLOCK OF ANGELS. 20

PINNED 22

SHE DREAMS OF RAVENS 23

IN THE TREES. 24

GRIEVING 25

DUSTY TEARS 26

HUNTING. 27

MELANCHOLY 28

FOUR WAYS 29

SATAN REBORN 30

ALL HER MORROWS 32

ALL HALLOW'S EVE 33

DOOMS 35

RAVEN-LASS ON PATROL 36

BEHOLD 37

COMING HOME 38

NATURAGENESIS 40

SHADOW PUPPETS 41

LOST AND FOUND 42

RENASCENCE 44

NEVADA TEST SITE MANNEQUINS 45

WORKING CLASS APOTHEOSIS 46

THE SONG OF RAIN 47

WHEN TEARS BLOOM 48

MIDNIGHT IN MOON ALLEY 49

NIGHT SWIMMERS 50

NIGHT BREED 52

HER PAIN 54

FLOWER MAID 55

THE SECRET PEOPLE 57

INSIDE 58

RAVEN 60

SHUNNED 61

DEFIANCE 63

AGING POET IN A SOHO TAVERN 64

THE DREAM 65

CARTOON HITMAN. 66

WILLOW 67

SEVERANCE 68

VANQUISHED. 69

WHERE THE ALICES GO 70

PAEAN FONCÉ AU CIEL 71

ELEMENTAL DISCOURSE. 72

THE RAIN HAS NO SHAMES 73

EDGAR 74

THE CAWING OF THE CROWS 77

LA PASSERELLE SYLVAN. 78

IMPRISONED 79

TO TRAVEL BY 80

BHÍ SÍ CAILLTE SNA VALES. 81

ALL THE LITTLE DEATHS 82

THUNDERBOLT. 83

LA BAIGNADE DANS L'OMBRE 84

CHILLIN'. 86

WISDOM FROM AN ITINERANT L.A. GURU 87

1,000 DAYS 88

THE TAPESTRY 91

FAMILIAR 93

UNBRIDLED HARBINGERS 94

DON'T FOLLOW 95

ALMOST 96

SO COLD 97

SHE CHOSE THE TRAIN 98

THE SCARLET HOOD 99

REST STOP 100

NOWHERE 101

POPPIN-JAY 102

AWAKEN 103

ON COAL MOUNTAIN 104

BLACK BIRD 105

A STRANGER 106

THE VOID 108

BEHIND THE DOOR 109

HOLDA 110

PRINCESS NIGHTFIRE 112

JOKER SELF PORTRAIT 113

MOTHER DAEMON 114

LOAMKIND 115

ANNA-LEE 118

FOREWORD

by Janet Morris

*"Sing to me, Muse," prayed the lyric
poets of ancient Greece.*

*"My words, though only breath,
are immortal," Sappho told us.*

*"Look, you," the earliest writers of the
Old Testament exhorted us.*

WHERE ARE TODAY'S LYRIC POETS? WHERE is today's Shelley? of whom critic and scholar Harold Bloom said: "His poetry has never had total appeal among literary people because it is idiosyncratic enough to be menacing."

Menacing. Hold that thought. That new voice is somewhere, lurking, even now. That menacing poet may well be in the pages of *DARK PARCHMENTS: Midnight Curses and Verses.*

Read and see.

And remember, as you do, the first lines of the Epic of Gilgamesh, written in the 18th century BCE, recently reconstructed by Theodore Kwasman as follows:

"Gilgamesh, who saw all, who was the foundation of the land,

"Who knew (everything), was wise in all matters."

Our poets, at their best, write our wisdom literature; at their worst, our baying at the moon. And with the vast outpouring of digital writings today, the great are swept along with the dross, into our own hands, where our eyes sort the best from the good and the worthless.

Rhyme? Blank verse? Free verse? All three carry our genetic need for rhyme, for rhythm, for song. Verse lodges in the memory and strikes the soul as nothing else can. We knew that once. The greats among our writers have always known it. The wildly revolutionary poets of the 17th and 18th centuries took poetry to its most dangerous heights. The "Beat" generation of the 20th century tried its best to follow.

Even today, the United States appoints a Poet Laureate, a tradition begun by European nations in the 14th century.

But where does poetry live among us now, in this age of truncated expression, greeting card sentiment, and 140-character quips? What relation has rap music to the Song of Solomon? or today's poets to the giants of literature? Only you can decide if the sonnets and other poems in *DARK PARCHMENTS: Midnight Curses and Verses* hold seeds of immortality in their lines.

One poem here is "*Awaken*." And so do we awaken, as we read its lines — to the menacing animus of this collection. These are dark poems, many atavistic, ambitious and harsh, some wrathful, some powerful, all uniquely modernist, as poets struggle to define their place in this century and tell the world their tales.

Another poem, "*The Song of Rain*, is slyly apocalyptic, as its author summons the rain to wash away all mankind's pain in an echo of the "Great Flood" lodged deep in our racial memory.

Gentility romps with madness in "*The Void*," a poem of everyday horror and 21st century angst.

And on we go, into a brooding anthology, into an adventure of minds exploring a central thesis: into humanity's awful heart, its crippling guilt and madness, its untoward dominion and unbridled power; even the catastrophes it creates — and due reckoning for its sins wreaked in this world and beyond.

"*Cartoon Hitman*" brings us a chilling taste of the untutored fury and proud violence native to the 21st-century American South, its vicious conceit creating a hater stalking cartoon heroes: "When I'm awound all cartoons hide. I pwactice animaticide."

"*Flower Maid*" calls a warning, whispers a cautionary tale from an imagined past, almost a fairy tale of Grimm's sort, with as dark a moral.

Read and discover not only these, but 80 more poems of bleakest nature — even three about nuclear terrors, mankind's latest phobia and modernity's most lasting fear.

The poems in *DARK PARCHMENTS: Midnight Curses and Verses* illuminate fears and horrors — but always, as with Shelley, idiosyncratically enough to be truly menacing.

— *Janet Morris, Cape Cod, 2015*

The Poems

GEHENNA DREAMS

SLIPP'RY AND SLIMY AND SLITH'RING
creeping and cravenly crawling
dripping and dragging and drooling
wickedly wilting and with'ring.

Scaly and scabby and screaming
hairy and hoary and hissing
cystic and cackling corrupting
stalking and sticking and stabbing.

Flapping and flaking and fleeing
plundered and plunging and pleading
crying and cracking and cringing
wraithfully wrathfully wailing!

Thus dark Gehenna dreams, beneath
the horrors of each human feat.

DOPPELGÄNGER

SHE SPIES HERSELF IN BROAD DAYLIGHT
knowing that nobody else sees
her doppelganger full of spite
and filling her with rank unease.

She knows that this double is real
and more than a mere reflection
with smiles not really quite ideal
and eyes empty of affection.

She sees it has more perfect skin
as if untouched by gravity
and reeks of some pact with dark sin
and horrific depravity.

She knows it wants to take her place
to live her life and wear her face.

THE FIRST WAVE

THEY ARE THE VERY FIRST OF ALL,
the ones who wait upon the gate
that separates heaven from hell
and all that's love from all that's hate.

They were the first to hurt and sin,
the first to spit on regency,
the front row of the closest kin
to creation's indecency.

They are the first wave of legions
to finally reach the border
of this farthest of hell's regions
in view of heaven's safe harbor.

And now their final punishment
eternity to stand and see
the matron
　　of their
　　banishment.

Remembrance

A REPORTER ASKED HIM OUTRIGHT
was his childhood really that bad
and were'nt his poems about that plight
really way too loathful and sad.

Surely his mother could not be
the ghoulish monster he described
and that cesspool on Clancy street
too outrageous can't be denied.

That hell of alcohol and smoke,
firetrap he managed to escape
so patently anti-baroque,
an origin tale ready made.

Orphaned poet flashed a wan smile
and bled a sigh 'neath haunted eye
empty of falsehood, hope, and guile.

HALLOWEENLAND

YES IT IS ALWAYS HALLOWEEN
in this particular nightmare
where no horror can be unseen
and every door leads to despair.

The trick or treaters are monsters,
the vilest creature's kith and kin
who serve the most wicked masters
born of all primordial sin.

Their costumes never can come off,
welded and sewn into their flesh,
each one a damned condemned seraph
long fallen from the ranks of blest.

The trick is its forever night
and all the treats are plague and blight.

She's Suffocating

SHE'S SUFFOCATING, CAN'T YOU SEE
the desperation in her eyes
filled with harsh tears like a black sea
brimming with dark and desperate lives.

She's suffocating, can't you hear
the panic in her muffled voice
knowing she soon will disappear
if she can't make the wisest choice.

She's suffocating, can't you feel
the fear residing in her soul,
the haunting threat that fate might steal
her chance for love and being whole.

Her time is quickly running out
as she battles this drowning doubt.

FLOCK OF ANGELS

I HAVE SEEN THEM CIRCLING THE EARTH,
vainly defying gravity,
gliding and soaring since the birth
of imperfect humanity.

Their wings have decayed through the years
abraded by the sins of man,
dark clouds of caustic hates and fears
that gnaw on them since life began.

Yet somehow they are still graceful,
these wounded avatars of old,
these wasting ranks of the faithful
judging us as our fates unfold.

At dusk I see their distant glint
their limbs of gold and hearts of flint.

PINNED

I AM PINNED TO THIS VERY SPOT,
nailed securely to sit and rot
by my weaknesses and my fears
leaving my spirit fraught and caught.

I'm pierced by everything I dread,
by visions unseen and unsaid
puncturing my too timid soul
whence all of my failed dreams have bled.

I'm haunted by these taut terrors
that punish me for my errors
that perforate and penetrate
just like life's most damning mirrors.

I wish I had the strength to rise
ripping all sin out of my skin
now free from all that I despise.

SHE DREAMS OF RAVENS

S HE DREAMS OF RAVENS EVERY NIGHT,
sometimes in droves, sometimes alone,
fluttering in their joyful flight,
whispering that she must atone

for a distant and ancient sin,
some harsh affront she blithely gave,
that she has long since forgotten
yet haunts her soul like lapping wave

returning so regularly,
splashing against her sleeping mind
with constant clawing urgency
that pains her as the ravens cry.

What is this guilt that so harries
within the seams of all her dreams
like strange dark-winged vigilantes.

IN THE TREES

GOD HEAR MY VOICE WITHIN THESE
scrawls
I pray that someone understands
I write my blood upon these walls
Petition of a hopeless man.

The treasure of my heart you see
She was my true and only love
And hand in hand she walked with me
Until Hell struck us from above.

No one believed my horrid claims
Too weirdly tragic without proof
When I awoke near her remains
The victim of scale, claw, and tooth.

Now soon they'll strap me to the chair
To blame for what is in the trees
"Avoid the park you must beware!"
I tear my throat with endless screams.

GRIEVING

SHE IS GRIEVING, FOR MANY THINGS
and so she wears an ivory veil
to mask the vile shadowy stings
contorting her face with a wail.

She is grieving for all the wars
and all of life's dark plundering,
the innocents who die in scores,
the survivors left suffering.

She is grieving for all the wrongs
a distant deity allows,
offering nothing but pale songs
that promise joy for keeping vows.

A deadly infectious sickness
her grief is too harsh to witness.

Dusty Tears

H AVE YOU EVER SEEN A DYING HOUSE CRY,
  its face covered in dusty tears,
all of its ancient wooden bones so dry
they creak and wail across the years.

Have you ever heard a dying house sing,
a dark and pitiful lament
oh so desperately trying to cling
to past glories now only dreamdt.

Have you ever felt a dying house shake
with shivers of stark loneliness,
abandoned by those who always forsake
the one who gave them childhood bliss.

Beside a lake it sadly fades
into memory's palest shades.

HUNTING

THIS RAVEN-HAIRED BEAUTY HAS PAUSED
midway in her dark reverie,
unaware she is slyly posed
as patiently predatory.

She licks and rubs her crimson lips
rich with the taste of wine's sweet bliss
as her candle flickers and drips
wax pale as her epidermis.

A haunting, shadowed loveliness,
practiced to keep the meek away,
desperate for a raw caress
and searching for love everyday.

Your gentle countenance she spies
out of the corner of her eyes.

MELANCHOLY

I THINK THAT MELANCHOLY IS
a young maid with silver-white locks,
a self-conscious and comely lass
drawn to embrace my darkest thoughts.

I think she lives in the shadows
of a haunting, distant forest
where no fair song ever echoes
and all joy is undernourished.

I think she should be avoided,
this siren shrouded in grey rain.
I know her beauty is poison
and sweet aspect my greatest bane.

She whispers to me every night,
lilting seduction I must fight.

Four Ways

Four ways of looking at mankind,
four paths for each of us to take,
four avatars inside our mind,
four visions that I just can't shake.

The first might open famine's door,
next non-stop waves of plagues release,
or endless all-consuming war
and most unlikely a world peace.

Each one a mere dice roll away,
each aching to express their song
with equal probability
that good intentions must go wrong.

They're waiting for life's next eclipse
four horsemen of apocalypse.

SATAN REBORN

HE IS UNFORMED AND INCOMPLETE,
floating in a maelstrom of dark,
a soul filled with destructive heat
wallowing like a drowning spark.

He's at the brink of consciousness,
struggling against a wave of dream
that drains his will and cognizance
as chaos and creation scream.

He aches and strains without breathing
though his heart fills to full expanse,
his spirit grows and starts teething
upon the cosmos' shadow dance.

He waits for an ebullient birth
upon a grand and glorious Earth.

ALL HER MORROWS

S HE'S STUCK INSIDE, SHE CAN'T GET OUT
and yes she really wants to leave
this gloomy domicile of doubt
that stains all she used to believe.

When she opens all of her doors
she's greeted by a wall of rain,
that darkness that all life abhors,
the vile essence of fear and pain.

Like iron bars this entity
contains and traps her deep inside
her flesh and blood identity
where her melancholies reside.

Each morn she peers out her windows
losing hope when seeing shadows,
the shades of failure and despair
condemning all of her morrows.

ALL HALLOW'S EVE

THREE NIGHTS BEYOND THE AUTUMN BOON
above a leaf forsaken tree
a rising moon will bleed the rune
and harbinger All Hallow's Eve.

Oh mothers hold your children close
and fathers fall to either knee
to pray that hosts of monster ghosts
will pass you by All Hallow's Eve.

Then keep the hearth a blazing pyre
for witches fly at night you see
and chimney fire appears too dire
for entry on All Hallow's Eve.

Prepare the scarecrow oh so vile
and jack-o-lantern jubilee
then light the smile that scares awhile
your sentinels All Hallow's Eve.

And finally the offerings
of honeyed sweets that parents leave,

the bribe for things that nighttime brings
placating ghouls All Hallow's Eve.

At last the very night is still
and all are home and safe asleep
bright candles fill each windowsill
protecting you All Hallow's Eve.

DOOMS

A RAVEN RAVES AND AN OWL HOWLS,
a craven jackal licks his jowls.
The spirits of the shadow folk
are prowling in their wailing cowls.
The moon is bleeding feral tears,
the stars are beads on mystic looms,
the world is drowning in its fears
and giving birth to runes and dooms.
Dark doorways open endlessly,
whirlpools in puddles beckoning,
ancient beseeching seraph songs
drum on and on and summon thee.

The hush of dusk is deafening,
the death of dawn dismembering.

Raven-Lass On Patrol

PERCHED HIGH, MANY MILES FROM
Gotham
nobly surveying road and tree
on lookout for the awful folk
who prey on innocents nightly.
She crouches down, coiling her legs
gripped firmly by ebony boots
and a long black leather duster
flapping so high above wormroots.
Her sister-soul, the crescent moon
slowly ascends a starry sky
as hoary hoots from hidden owls
alert her that evil is nigh.

Her lips stretch in a feral grin,
dark predator awaiting sin.

BEHOLD

BEHOLD THE WIZARDS OF THIS CENTURY
just aching to dispense their alchemy,
casting a spell of dark ebullience,
casting a spell to set a dragon free.

Behold their tragic anticipation,
their breathless salivating reverie
drunk on the brandy of their creation
with hearts pounding in proud fecundity.

Behold this celestial explosion
so shocking in all of its raw beauty,
an infant star breaching the horizon,
the blast of winds a haunting birthing scream.

COMING HOME

I'M A CELTIC SONG OF THE WHISP'RY TREES
on a Limerick path near a laughing stream,
I am ghost, and soul, and vision, and tease,
I am raw mirage, wild and willowy.

Astride pale horse, silent as a breeze,
amidst rolling waves of lilting lilies,
we splash through the buzz of sweet honey bees,
tangy dandelions, and morning glories.

Keeping pace with the skies dark sorcery
we're racing a dawn bronze and coppery
for day's blinding eye is a harsh disease
to all of the eldritch folk of faerie.

Oh we're almost there, 'neath the branches sleeves
and the sylvan mists and the amber leaves.

NATURAGENESIS

I KEEP HEARING ABOUT BEARS BREAKING
into homes,

deer causing automobile accidents,

bird strikes bringing airplanes down,

shark attacks close to the beach,

forest fires devouring neighborhoods,

floods overcoming towns, and

hurricanes devastating coastal communities.

I think nature has commenced its counter-attack.

SHADOW PUPPETS

YOU FIND ME WANDERING, IN SEARCH OF
love
across a landscape of shadow puppets
happily grafted to transitory
marionette strings of wealth/fame/beauty.
I try to touch one, but meet emptiness;
a hollow construct of breathless voices,
shallow paper plaything lacking substance,
oblivious to flesh and blood appeals.
So I pen my songs of simple whimsy
ignored by twilight wraiths with tin toy ears,
excelsior guts, icy dead doll eyes;
callous automatons of ambition.

I am alone on this silent playground.
Tell me, where do the other children go?

LOST AND FOUND

THEY KEPT SAYING IT WAS ONE NIGHT
and he just screamed right back at them
that he'd been lost twenty fortnight
pursued by a monstrous mayhem.

They laughed and said that he was drunk
when chased into the dark forest,
a fool demanding one more drink
who fled their fist and feet's torrent.

He yelled he entered some hell land
filled with creatures vicious and wild
and every day he near went mad
battling these demons he had riled.

He'd lived on roots and foul water,
not sleeping for more than an hour
avoiding a pending slaughter
in this eternal night's bower.

Yes that was right, there was no sun
in this curst and horrific place

and no matter how far he'd run
the moon above always kept pace.

Until just now with this escape
but they guffawed at his feigned awe
cowering to their every jape.

RENASCENCE

THIS WONDER OF THE MODERN WORLD,
this generation's colossus,
phantasm of nightmares unfurled
and product of brute sub conscience.

Behold the living rising god
of elemental destruction
that dares to reach right up and prod
Heaven's very own construction.

Just stand in awe of this power,
gaze now upon primal fury,
witness this primeval flower
blossoming with dark ecstasy.

Nevada Test Site Mannequins

WHO YOU CALLING DUMMY, DUMMY?
Surely not my infant and me
crouching fearfully in basement,
cowering oh so helplessly.
No we're not just useless puppets
or playthings to amuse all thee
who shiver as you pass us by
feeling strangely oddly guilty.
Do not debase my frozen beauty
framed by this grey concrete cellar
artistically arbitrary
and soon to be rendered stellar.

Go now and please just let us be.
We're haunted by a blinding dream.

WORKING CLASS APOTHEOSIS

OH MY GOD, JUST WHAT HAVE WE DONE
besides turning the night to day
and giving birth to nascent sun
and crossing under hell's archway.

Surely we can't be doing this,
ripping into reality,
unholy apotheosis,
amoral creativity.

We've torn a gap into chaos,
a door to dark, shadowy realms
that makes me wonder what we've lost
as all this power overwhelms.

Perhaps the first deific crime
we've violated space and time.

THE SONG OF RAIN

THE RAIN, THE RAIN, THE RAMMING
slamming rain,
it's wondrous might and sheer delight exclaimed,
cacophony and symphony
composed, arranged epiphany
and wet applause for all of mankind's banes.

The dripping, dropping, wishy-washy rain,
this fickle trickle wildly unrestrained.
The splish and splash of water play
the curse of every holiday
I wish it rained each night and day
until the whole world washed away
and cleansed the earth of all its pain.

And this is why I now proclaim
the humming, drumming song of rain,
the rain, the damning dinning rain!

WHEN TEARS BLOOM

WHEN HER TEARS BLOOM, HER GRIEF
flowers,
exposing a loamy beauty
trickling down in salty showers
when her life gets grey and moody
and her dark destiny glowers
and sadness blinds her to duty,
when her tears bloom, her grief flowers.

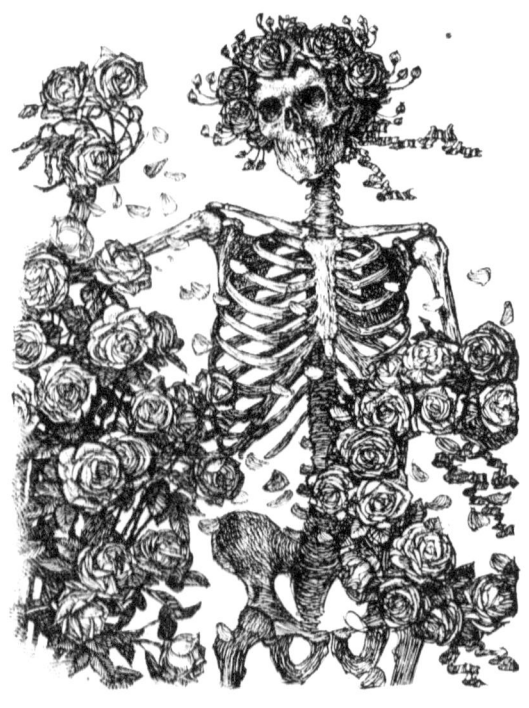

MIDNIGHT IN MOON ALLEY

WE JOURNEY THROUGH ENDLESS ALLEYS
Bathed in moonlight, led by candles
Speaking in whispers, wispy and soft
Holding hands, smiling in shadows
The warmth of night clutching our breasts
Our footsteps as light as cats' feet
We float and flow through the city
Dream-like serpent of human flesh
A living train of such dark will
Our blush heralds our arrival
Strange angels greet us
    with their song.

NIGHT SWIMMERS

S HE IS A CREATURE OF WATER
wading through tidings and greetings
unaffected by the currents
of shallow, chill conversations.

The warmth of laughter draws her near,
luring her with a full chuckle,
enticing glow of ruddy blush
and the scent of frank loneliness.

Calmly, quietly she drifts close,
preternatural gaze,
entrancing and mesmerizing,
quickly startling and capturing.

Floating in wispy greens and blues
and all of fate's rapacious hues.

NIGHT BREED

EMERGING FROM DEEPEST DARKNESS
Fey creature of sapphire shadows
Freckled in moonlight and star shine
Painted nocturnal reflections
And the patterns of living night
Your beauty is a siren song
Your lips a soft rosy whisper
Your almond eyes searching, searching
Both telling me and asking me
Seeing inside, looking straight through
Preternatural, uncanny
Innocent and then judgmental
Strange and beautiful chimera
Unearthly dream made spectral flesh
Daring me, taunting me, to wake.

HER PAIN

NOBODY SEES HER PAIN, HIDDEN
in shadows and behind closed doors,
sequestered inside of four walls
and a roof of oppressive shames.

Nobody hears her pain, swallowed
by pale, uncaring silences,
a holocaust of harsh stillness,
a crass stupefying vacuum.

Nobody feels her pain, the aches
and jabs, punctures, and raw tearing
psychic wounds in a mortal soul,
helpless, shivering, wallowing.

Her pain is real, a beast that clings
where spirit wails, and horror sings.

Flower Maid

THE LEGEND OF THE FLOWER MAID
all grandmothers just ache to tell
to naughty, spiteful pretty girls
who yearn to be a ballroom belle.

There was a vain and lovely child
who treated others with disdain
demanding daily the worship
of captain, cook, and chatelaine.

She used her charms in petty ways
to garner sweets and praise and lace
and bade that all village damsels
parade behind her one full pace.

Until that day she came of age
insisting that every flower
within the county-wide domain
be plucked for her jubilant hour.

And so fetching was this cute miss
that all the gardens were defaced

with not a single window pot
left for any sill to embrace.

She sang and danced through the town square
upon a hill of fresh cut blooms,
when all the blossoms came to life
and all her beauty was consumed.

They say trees whisper late at night
the dark fate of that comely lass
whose efflorescent ghost now seeks
all gorgeous girls selfish and crass.

The Secret People

CAN YOU SEE THE SECRET PEOPLE
     painted in all the hues of night,
a mellifluous camouflage
immune to all but second sight?

Have you heard the secret people
whispering in every shadow
that flickers gently at your feet,
trembling 'neath dusk's sweet afterglow?

Have you felt the secret people
whose touch the soft caress of wind
teases the soul of each artist
with all the temptations of sin?

Adorned in mauve and ebony
and hidden shrouds of harmony.

INSIDE

C AN YOU FEEL THE HURT, DEEP INSIDE,
    well hidden from harsh prying eyes
where all my dark secrets reside
behind bright amber walls of lies.

Can you hear the hurt echoing
through my empty hollowed out soul
and forever resonating
after each hope that life just stole.

Can you see the hurt, deep within
flowing back and forth through my veins
a tide of unrelenting sin
teeming with love's rapacious banes.

Why can't you strip away my flesh
and witness all that I suppress.

RAVEN

TWO PIERCING EYES OF GLISTENING NIGHT
'pon noble brow both wise and bold,
evocative of mythic might,
sung by brave warriors of old.

Rangy raptor in plucky plume
of ancient, savage, sky-born breed,
a proud visage cloaked in fierce gloom
and mystic shades of ebony.

Graceful nocturnal sovereign,
phantasmal grandiosity,
you spin like wraith, dervish, and jinn
within a churning, star-filled sea.

Thus crowned dauntless, corvine monarch,
trickster, portent, Prince of the dark.

SHUNNED

I AM THE OLD MAN WHO IS SHUNNED,
the useless relative, abhorred,
the harbinger from which kids run,
pariah of the mistutored.

My mere presence embarrasses,
my voice makes everybody cringe,
spawn of discrepant marriages
forever waiting on the fringe.

Wrongly libeled, unfairly feared,
strangely unappreciated,
a scary clown all youth have jeered
fated to be scorned and hated.

I am Death, the bringer of peace
the end of pain, life's sweet release.

DEFIANCE

I WILL NOT LET MY DEATH TAKE FLIGHT,
I shall not stop grasping his leash,
I'm far too young to end this fight
between release and disbelief.

My weakness will not conquer me
though my own heart and lungs betray
my efforts to arise and breathe
while shutting out all those who pray.

I fear the pleasant cloak of night
which my naked soul aches to wear
and shan't shed this most crippling fright
that threatens me with dark despair.

I won't give up, I shall defy
this damning urge to sleep and fly.

Aging Poet In a Soho Tavern

"I AM POETRY," HE SHOUTED
pounding back another foul shot
and slamming fist on bar, pouted,
beseeching one more glass of rot.

"My blood is fire, my bones are earth,"
then he belched, and coughed, and spat phlegm
on scarred oak floors with crusty mirth,
"New York critics, fuck all of 'em."

Next, he shook and began to cry
big thick tears like late autumn rain,
blew his nose on sleeve with a whine,
"college pricks know shit about pain."

He dropped my textbook at my feet
and staggered back onto the street.

The Dream

EACH DUSK HER NIGHTMARE STARTS THE same,
she's stranded in a forest vale,
half naked without any shame,
an actress in a dark folktale.

Her skirt extends beyond her sight,
its weight hampers her every stride,
fleeing foul things bathed in moonlight
and horrors from which she can't hide.

They crawl and scamper in pursuit,
manifestations of her dread
and guilt that bears the fetid fruit
of one whose soul has wept and bled.

She trips and then is overcome
waking and screaming 'neath the sun.

CARTOON HITMAN

BUGS BUNNY FAILED MY WABBIT TEST
his wucky foot hangs on my chest.
And that star-belly Sneetch who snitched
I pitched headwess into a ditch.

Yes Daffy's wisp dwove me insane
I pushed that qwack out of a pwane.
And Popeye's stutter ticked me off
siwenced by my Kawishnikov.

He drawled too slow that southern hound
so I had huckleberry dwowned.
Magilla did not take the hint
his hands and feet sold for a mint.

When I'm awound all cartoons hide.
I pwactice animaticide.

WILLOW

SHE'S LIKE A TREE THAT GROWS AND grieves,
one swaying in a hurricane,
bent over as she barely breathes,
uprooted by a baleful bane.

Her tears stream down like bloody sap,
burning her eyes, blurring her sight
and with fate's every thunderclap
she's damned with an internal blight.

Her beauty is an autumn crown
bejeweled with prismatic leaves,
but like a bride stripped of her gown
she suffers pain that claws and cleaves.

Her sorrow and her agony
are seedlings of life's travesty.

Severance

SHE THINKS SHE'S DISINTEGRATING
One small particle at a time
A slow painless dissipating
So sad and hopelessly sublime

Avoiding all of the hating
And starvation, and horrid crime
And endless sins so damaging
To all that's precious and divine

That her gentle heart starts breaking
And her soul can no longer shine
She thinks she's disintegrating.

VANQUISHED

MEOWSKAVITZ AND HIS ROBOT
are conquering across the earth
and repeating like a parrot,
"humans must bow to our mad mirth!"

Breaking buildings, toppling towers,
robotic Ralph is rampaging
with orders from his meower's
psychic helmet now transmitting

only quick capitulation
to this kitty conquistador
will guarantee that his mission
ends its destruction evermore.

So surrender you fine people,
drop down onto a wobbly knee
and pledge that cats are your equal
from now unto eternity.

Where The Alices Go

WHERE DO ALL THE ALICES GO,
the ones who daily disappear,
one moment here, next I don't know,
fleeting as a taut, timid deer.

How do the Alices vanish
in this world of science and facts,
what cold government would banish
them in dark, clandestine attacks.

Why do the Alices depart,
not telling any guardian
or family close to their heart
reasons they'd run away again.

What cave or looking-glass doorway
or tempting gem has swallowed them
spiriting off to far away.

Paean Foncé au Ciel

SHE WONDERS WHY NO ONE LISTENS
as her cries have risen to screams
and her form glows bright and glistens
above her maltreated remains.

She ponders why no one shows grief,
not cop or ambulance driver,
one who stole her life like a thief,
or even jaded grave digger.

She saunters the cemetery,
leaving no imprint on the ground,
ignored by the sedentary
souls that seem to sleep safe and sound.

Her stone is marked 'unknown, unloved'
an unfair brand and damning ban
barring a junkie from above.

ELEMENTAL DISCOURSE

SHE SAYS, "MORTALS ARE ONE MORE GIFT."
Then 'she' replies, "they are a curse"
"and we ought to make their end swift."
Quite shocked SHE blurts back, "you're the worst!"

Surprised, 'she' adds, "they poison Earth."
Smiling SHE says, "but some fight back"
"and struggle to give it rebirth."
"Too late," 'she' snipes, "since their attack."

"All life is sacred," SHE intones.
"They slaughter species," 'she' replies,
"turning all life to dust and bones."
SHE whispers, "yes, I've heard their cries."

And looking in each other's eyes
they contemplate mankind's demise.

The Rain Has No Shames

THE RAIN HAS NO SHAMES, NONE AT ALL,
when it falls it causes such pain,
so fierce it can topple a wall,
from rage it will never abstain.

The rain has no fear, not within,
nothing deters or makes it pause,
it is a most relentless Djinn
with tiny catastrophic claws.

The rain has no mercy, or reprieve,
nor pity for those in its sway,
using both good and bad to weave
tapestries of all it can slay.

It is the coldest of all flames,
a sopping soul, it has no shames.

EDGAR

THE PATRON SAINT OF DARK DESPAIR,
the depthless gloom of your pale stare,
your spirit guide a black raven,
dour troubadour with sable hair.

The loss of love so innocent
you drowned in sins pure and potent,
haunted by fame's indifference,
left broken and recalcitrant.

Your poems are rashly radiant
with visions you could not repent,
wailing in the depths of sadness,
transcendent and grandiloquent.

Mad, murky Edgar Allen Poe
you saw beyond what mere men spawned
shadowy grandfather of woe.

The Cawing of The Crows

I FEEL ITS TRUE, THOUGH NO ONE KNOWS
those fleeting forms like black arrows
are harbingers of cessation,
I fear the cawing of the crows.

I hear them sleeping, and awake,
fluttering high, like thin dark clouds
and know that they will not forsake
this chance to spread their dismal shrouds.

They know the path that I have trod
and all my unrepentant sins,
glaring right through my thin façade,
spreading their wings like assassins.

Creatures born of scornful shadows
they come for me
'pon midnight's sea
honor guards to my soul's gallows.

La Passerelle Sylvan

IS THERE A DOORSILL IN THE WOODS,
one not wedded to house or shed,
unknown by nearby neighborhoods
where one can flee from every dread?

Is there a leaf-shrouded
    threshold,
a timeworn, mystic
    passageway,
a safe respite that was
    foretold
far from any street or
    highway?

Is there an odd and eldritch arch
made of moss-stained granite and oak,
seen only by moonlight or torch
when victims beg, pray, and invoke?

Will ley line paths or gold brick roads
please show the ways to better days
through doorways sung in ancient odes.

Imprisoned

I DWELL INSIDE A GILDED CAGE,
a den both humble and demure,
walls covered in the sweet plumage
of artistry pleasing and pure

comforting and distracting me
from all of life's enduring fears,
confined in bulwarks of beauty
my ego slowly disappears

into a thick and hardened shell
impervious to any threat,
a charming, soporific spell
and limping, loving, living death.

To Travel By

I'VE BEEN JOURNEYING, OFF THE ROAD
between some places, off the grid,
locale to locale, no payload
traveling light, far from fervid.

I have not been in a hurry
since that time that I lost my way,
not feeling panic or worry
I walk nonstop without dismay.

It's always neither night nor day
as I never see sun or moon,
the sky is always maudlin grey,
I never need to rest or swoon.

I don't remember when or why
with no omen or sweet harken
I chose this hell to travel by.

BHÍ SÍ CAILLTE SNA VALES

THEY SAY SHE'S LOST IN THE HEATHER,
others, some lover did her in,
an irish lass without trespass,
much to the constable's chagrin.

It was getting late in autumn,
when sheep coats are not far from thin,
and the dark sky betrayed a cry,
the distant call of scared maiden.

The village searched each farm and dale
and every single stream and brook,
yet found no trace of freckled face
or reason why she was forsook.

It is a Gaelic mystery
why this sweet dame of fiery mane
fell victim to skullduggery.

ALL THE LITTLE DEATHS

T O GOD, LIFE IS ONE LONG AUTUMN
filled up with all the little deaths,
each one a blossoming phantom
allotted mere handfuls of breaths.

THUNDERBOLT

WAS IT A DREAM OR A VISION,
maybe just one, or perhaps both
burned in my mind with precision
and beautiful, I'd swear an oath.

Passing right by my rear window,
captured by a flash of lightning,
eyes a green incandescent glow,
mesmerizing and frightening.

And just as quickly she was gone,
this lovely multi-colored wraith
whose scarlet lips and black locks spawn
desires that challenge all my faith.

This stormy midnight fantasy
savages and ravishes me.

LA BAIGNADE DANS L'OMBRE

S HE LAVES IN A SPICY DARKNESS,
caressed by soft, sable lappings
of luxuriating blackness,
snugly warm in shadowed wrappings.

Her aspect still and saturnine,
her smile both secret and arcane
with locks a lovely ebony
eclipsing eyes of porcelain.

Her movements are slow and dusky,
reflecting naught but murky light
releasing breaths sweet and musky
deep into this ebullient night.

Her guise is lavender and lush
glowing with midnight's darksome blush.

Chillin'

YEAH, I'VE BEEN HANGING WITH SHADOWS,
marking time in the dim twilight,
swapping signs with shady fellows
and riding pumpkins at midnight.

They are darklings of after dusk,
unfamiliars to all day-kind,
tall groovy gusts of sable dust
phasing in and out of my mind.

We sidestep all the luminous,
evading the incandescent,
mainlining the mysterious
and battling with the quiescent.

I want to become one of them
nobody's fool tripping on cool
free of life's mad, maudlin mayhem.

WISDOM FROM AN ITINERANT L.A. GURU

ALL MY LIFE I'VE FOLLOWED A CROOKED path,

and my guardian angel was a sociopath,

my guardian angel was a sociopath.

That's right Joes, the harper's shop gonna close

and losers like you will truly get hosed

and my guardian angel lost his wings,

my guardian angel did evil things.

Forgive me lad but you've been had,

Robinson's saucer left this take-off pad,

atomic rockets coughing hot rad,

and that is bad, man, really really bad.

Cuz my guardian angel was so vain,

my guardian angel was insane,

he was, he was, he transcended this plane,

leaving me behind in the acid rain.

1,000 Days

FOUND IN A FORGOTTEN BOOKSTORE

just off route one in central Maine

She read a long, bygone ballad

between many a crumbling page

about a Welsh poet who spent

one day trapped in a strange garden

'pon straying from his caravan

not far from ancient Canaan

after daring Aphrodite

during a reckless, drunken binge

to grant him the truth of women

and 'pon escape he wrote this lay

about his odd duration there

for him one thousand eldritch days

spent with one thousand maidens fair

while outside that plot's tall stone walls

only a single day had passed

as each morn one maid filled a door

an arch that was not there before

to spend a full day just with him

trading stories, songs, and kisses

til night when each beauty faded
like mist dispersed upon the wind
and his description of each lass
had such a wealth of fine details
that She soon came to realize
described ladies of every class
from lots of different decades
from separate countries and lands
of every race and every age
before and after his lifespan
who wrote this poem so long ago
before the phone or radio
and then She read of his last day
the thousandth in this lush garden
that though feeding him o'er two years
had left this Welshman drawn and thin
when the last damsel came within
a lovely lass, colonial
with chestnut hair and emerald eyes
perfect pale skin and scarlet lips
with pretty smile sad eyes belied
like all her life had been decreed
to search the world's end just for he
and on this day they shared a love

a warm, never-ending release
that granted both of them sweet peace
and then She knew that She was she
the sad, lonely colonial
the last time-traveler he kissed
when freed upon the final line
of this verse of unearthly bliss.

Thus She came to Lebanon's shores
and now searches across each day
for that miraculous garden
and vine-clad, enchanted doorway.

The Tapestry

SHE REMEMBERS WHEN SHE WAS YOUNG,
exploring her rich aunt's attic,
finding a tapestry well spun
of some luminescent fabric.

Pressing against it she soon gasps
passing through fibers like a mist
out of a cave to magic lands
and everything she ever wished.

And after many wondrous years,
a lady, she entered that cave
and emerged as a child in tears
onto a field and her aunt's grave.

She finds one hundred years have fled
since her own parents passed away
and none believe her tale of dread,
thinking her some waif led astray.

Decades later she spends her life
struggling to find that tapestry

hoping to escape years of strife
back to her youth and family.

FAMILIAR

S HE WAKES ME NOT LONG AFTER DUSK,
feeding on all radiant light
and speaks to my soul on the cusp
of each full moon upon midnight.

She whispers shadowy secrets
and truths I almost cannot bear,
held in the heart of the deepest
of every sin's ebony lair.

She spreads her wings and bids me fly
with her into life's endless night
and thus decry a starry sky,
screaming a song of dark delight.

Her eyes, black pearls, are tempting me
to strip my skin
and free my sin
with bold, ebullient beauty.

UNBRIDLED HARBINGERS

I HEAR THE HORSES THUNDERING
not far beyond forever's cusp,
a faint drum that keeps echoing
and charging towards the coming dusk.

At first I only knew their song
within my deepest darkest dreams,
then when adulthood came along
it bled through my waking world's seams.

Now every day I sit dismayed
that no one else takes note of them,
all unaware of booming neigh,
ignorant of what they condemn.

Soon they will trample all our lies
judging the sin
of all our kin
oblivious to pleas and cries.

DON'T FOLLOW

SUCH LONG DARK LOCKS AND PALE SKIN
could not help but arrest my eyes
within a chilly autumn wind
on the edge of the forest rise.

She seemed to be beckoning me
beyond the pine trees and the oaks
through pallid mists, 'cross musky leaf,
her every step a tempting coax.

And then she suddenly vanished
within a patch of grey heather
where I found bones scattered and blanched
in the same yet shredded sweater.

Beware of secrets nature yields
where darkness creeps and never sleeps.
Avoid the moors, meadows, nettles,
spurn what every spectre shields
and don't follow phantoms through fields.

ALMOST

I ONCE CAUGHT DEATH FLIRTING WITH ME
out of the corner of my eye
when I began to fall asleep
on a park bench in New Jersey.

It was a cold winter morning
after a long and bitter fight
that lasted nearly all the night
forgetting who was wrong or right.

The moon had set, the sun still slept
the dark chill quickly filling me
when a sweet voice offered escape
from all my life's harsh misery.

Her kiss almost touched my forehead
a sweet caress she ached to press
but I awoke to fight my dread
wishing to rise from wormwood's bed,
I chose to wake and live, instead.

So Cold

S O COLD, SO COLD, SO VERY COLD,
harshly unremittingly cold,
cold old man winter never sold,
crippling the boldest of the bold.

Cold that chills her right to the bone,
cold that trickles throughout her soul,
cold that makes her feel all alone,
cold that defies the hottest coal.

So cold it is a kind blessing,
an imperfect yet callous cure
freezing the pain of suffering
with icy fingers pale and pure.

Now safe within this castled cold
where she can flee society
like veils of thick, inert white gold.

She Chose The Train

A LOVELY VISION, YES SHE WAS
with pale skin and raven mane,
without a witness or applause
she jumped the stile and chose the train.

She could have picked a simple bridge
or a towering skyscraper
or flown her car into a ditch
or some other fatal caper.

But no, she chose to take the train,
grand symbol of another age,
a supreme shot of Novocain
to instantly end all her pain.

An unhappy soul is destroyed
as train and miss both share a kiss
and flesh and steel enter the void.

The Scarlet Hood

WHAT HAPPENED TO RED RIDING HOOD,
you know she was misunderstood,
not quite so innocent and frail
as in that biased fairy tale.

And was that wolf really so bad
and was he really such a cad.
His wife and kids had to be fed,
that's what the naturalist said.

You know Riding Hood's scarf was white
until that horrid bloody night
her lover the lumberjack bade
to kiss the wolf's neck with his blade.

Don't be fooled by her pretty face
it just might hide dire lupuscide
and terrors it fains to embrace.

REST STOP

SHE IS A SCARY ALIEN,
I think she wants to eat my heart,
perfect for soup or sandwiches
for denizens of planet Splort.

She descended just this morning,
twitching her nose, licking her lips,
two actions that cannot fool me,
she's looking for a tasty dish.

Her voice-box says she comes in peace,
her gaze says I'm a smorgasbord,
her smile so sweet and innocent,
she'd shish kabob me that's for sure.

Late for breakfast, early for lunch
this cute E.T. is eyeing me.
Yes, maybe its my faulty hunch
and she likes humans a whole bunch
but I think she landed for brunch
and in the mood to munch and crunch!

NOWHERE

I REMEMBER THAT UNCANNY DAY
as if it were just yesterday
when she suddenly disappeared,
somehow spirited far astray.

A summer picnic in a field
that stretched as far as eyes can see,
where grass and flowers have revealed
a dark and heartless mystery.

Her cry was sudden and a shock,
sounding a dozen yards away,
which spooked and startled a nighthawk
that screamed and fled in dire dismay.

Hundreds then scoured the dour meadow,
finding neither quicksand nor lair
as if she had become shadow
dismissed by sunlight to nowhere.

Years later her scream still haunts me
as I ponder and then conjure
what was the last thing she could see.

POPPIN-JAY

WHAT HAPPENED TO THAT ODD AU PAIR,
   the posh one with an umbrella,
the bog trotter with a false air
of public school Cinderella.

Last seen walking out of some flat
into a rough and wintry storm
like some malformed raven with hat
quickly engulfed by snowflake swarm.

It's said she was quite a songstress,
warbler to the highest degree,
though emotionally a mess,
a wacky OCD banshee.

Beware nannies who advocate
a happenstance
and song and dance
home-schooling in the first estate.

AWAKEN

LORD WAKE ME FROM THIS HORRID DREAM
this nightmare whence I'm wallowing
this empty stagnant hollowing
which sickens with its fouling
and slavering and swallowing
this horror that is following
and burrowing and howling!

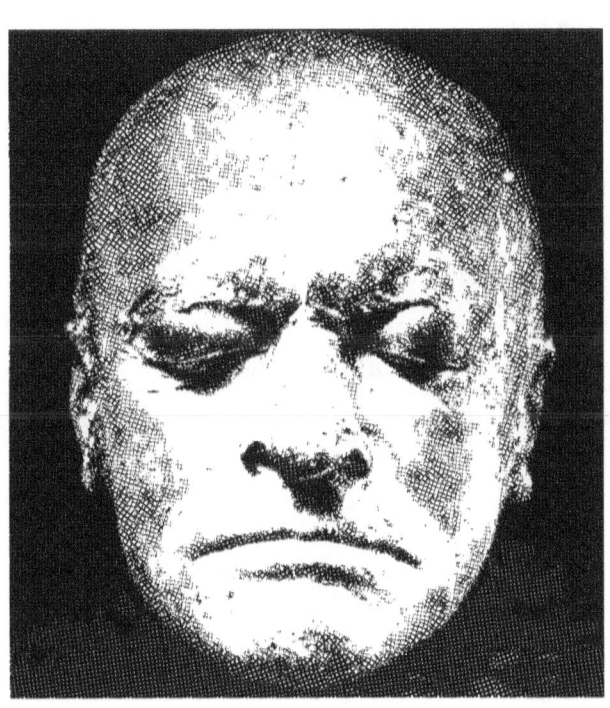

ON COAL MOUNTAIN

JUST ONE MORE DAY ON COAL MOUNTAIN
choking on time's corrosive dust,
a hot, hellishly coarse fountain
of sad, bubbling, ebony rust.

The cuts and scars along her limbs
speak of a dark and horrid life
scaling this proof of mankind's sins
upon the blue sky's tortured wife.

She slumps in momentary pause
struggling to master all her pain,
exhausted on these feral claws
of anthracite and human bane.

She wipes black tears off of her face
knowing they always leave a trace.

BLACK BIRD

THE BLACK BIRD FEASTS ON ALL OF US,
from birth and throughout all our life,
using one to a thousand cuts
made with its hooked and amber knife.

The black bird is up in the skies,
watching every adult and child,
judging with its all-knowing eyes,
claiming both worthy and reviled.

The black bird is not of this world
and yet it is Earth's eldest kin,
whose ebony wings first unfurled
when mankind chose to commit sin.

The blackbird perches by our head
the only friend on our deathbed.

A STRANGER

A STRANGER CAME INTO MY HOME
and asked me if I was alive
so I sung softly for my soul
which promptly came right back inside.

A stranger paced me in a park
and asked me if I'd passed away
so I whispered my spirit hark
and return, having gone astray.

A stranger swam right next to me
and asked me if I was dying
so I let my ghost know my need
as I lay floating in the sea.

Some might fear what his words portend
odd outlander, shadowed stranger
yet I think of him as my friend.

THE VOID

H AVE YOU HEARD THE CALL OF THE VOID,
have you tasted its pleasant song
when you're in pain, or unemployed
or suffering an unfair wrong.

Oh have you felt the void's caress,
the welcome itch of its tickle,
the promise of its charming kiss
when fleeing the vain and fickle.

Yes have you seen it beckoning
with both its distant pale hands
offering a fair reckoning
of all you endured in harsh lands.

And now my soul wants to avoid
all thoughts of when I clasped the void
or left it clutching my spirit
no, I can't remember that bit,
leaving me so strangely annoyed,
and my mind keeps wanting to drift...
perhaps I'm still inside of it.

BEHIND THE DOOR

I'M WAITING NOW, BEHIND THIS DOOR,
waiting for you forevermore,
patiently penning pale poems
that you just might perchance adore.

I'm nesting here, behind this door,
not far from the songs of seashore,
dreaming of your alluring eyes
that rival goddesses of yore.

I'm drifting now, behind this door,
safe from sickness, danger, and war,
humming an ode to shrouded trysts
wafting among these charming mists.

Behind this door, behind these walls
please hear my voice, pray heed my calls.

HOLDA

I DREAMT ABOUT PERLACHER FORST,
the realm I lived in as a child
where climbing trees fulfilled my thirst
in the raw beauty of the wild.

And in this coniferous trance,
this leafy, musky phantasy,
amidst the songbirds and the ants
I chanced 'pon sweet tranquility.

A creature both silent and fey,
grey eyes so preternatural
with chestnut hair in disarray,
flirtatious and baldly bashful.

Her aspect was a question mark,
a strange will-o'-the-wisp-like plea
implying I had come to shirk
some long-forgotten destiny.

Then I awoke in dire dread
failing to grasp some fleeting task
like the end of an unspooled thread.

Princess Nightfire

S HE IS SEEN VERY LATE AT NIGHT,
running through the fringe villages
of India beneath moonlight
crowned in the fire that pillages.

Her aspect no one can describe,
her guise is clothed in holy flames,
her escort a radiant hive
of Hummas bled from the sky's veins.

She is neither evil nor good,
but a goddess of yesteryear,
adorned in her bright, cosmic hood,
spreading a wondrous, haunting fear.

Dark nature's ancient defiance
a force of will spirits distill
beyond logic and staid science.

Joker Self Portrait

THE BATMAN PUT ME BEHIND BARS
for just one innocent antic,
tying a bad Judge to two cars,
then watched them split, do you get it?

The Batman beat me horribly,
punching me with his big black fist,
I set the zoo's polar bear free
on an ice cream social, get it?

The Batman chased me for two hours
after leaving that famed dentist
and swapping all his teeth with flowers,
a screaming violet, get it?

I pray you like my work of art,
though it gave the Docent a fit,
that sensitive and bleeding heart,
only palette in sight, get it?

MOTHER DAEMON

SHE IS THE MOTHER OF DAEMONS
sowing eldritch legions,
she is the widow of chieftains
and the blight of seasons.

She rules not far beneath the earth,
eating moonlight and rain,
nature's only true virgin birth
and dreams are her domain.

She suckles mankind's every joy
with the milk of reason,
dangling it like a precious toy
and forbidden treason.

Her dark, maternal fingers play
across the breast of every day.

LOAMKIND

I N THE RIVER VALLEY,
Along the forest edge,
You should not wander far
For there are things to dread;
Darklings, shadow things
Strange shapes that undulate,
Vapory and willowy
With eyes that glow in wait.

Beneath, behind waterfalls
Its said they have their lairs
And rest in green puddle-beds
On sacks filled with frog hairs.
They sleep all day
Under a bright stalactite lamp
Which warms their soggy hearts
And souls so damp.

They hunger for months
And wait for the right time
When naughty boys and girls
Must pay for a crime.

Perhaps for stealing
Or telling a lie,
Hurting a little sibling
Squashing a butterfly.

They'll enter from a basement
Or the chimney,
One way or another
When the stars wink dimly.
They'll smell your badness
And all of your wrong
And no blanket will stop them,
They are much too strong.

They'll drag you into darkness
To work in their mine
Harvesting pale mushrooms
To soak in barrels of brine.
And if you're lucky
You might escape one day
To tell this wild story
While folks call you crazy.

In the river valley,
Along the forest edge,

You should not wander far

For there are things to dread;

Darklings, shadow things

Strange shapes that undulate

Vapory and willowy

With eyes that glow in wait.

ANNA-LEE

OCTOBER BREEDS A LONELY EVE
as wounded hearts sublimely bleed
upon this anniversary
of Death embracing Anna-Lee.

This very hour twelve moons ago
my heart was cruelly torn from me
as land's majestic ancient foe
unfairly claimed my Anna-Lee.

Oh God forgive my stupid dare
Forgive our foolish moonlit spree
a soul consumed by dark despair
and endless grief for Anna-Lee.

She took my challenge on that shore
and dove into that shadowed sea
and like an ancient castle door
the water closed on Anna-Lee.

Oh brazen reckless mortal man
oh spawn of stale mortality

left screaming on that horrid sand
forever reft of Anna-Lee.

Each day I drown in Devil's brew
reliving my weak fatal deed
and resurrecting all I rue
my long lost lover Anna-Lee.

Oh Anna-Lee, sweet Anna-Lee
each night I waken to my scream
and wander back down to the sea
where I last held you Anna-Lee.

Bright silver waves reflect the moon
and offer up pale hands to me
sweet promise of a gentle doom
uniting me with Anna-Lee.

- THE END -

About the Poet

Michael H. Hanson is the Creator of the Sha'Daa shared-world, horror/fantasy anthology series currently consisting of *Sha'Daa: Tales of The Apocalypse, Sha'Daa: Last Call, Sha'Daa: Pawns, Sha'Daa: Facets,* and the soon to premiere *Sha'Daa: Inked* all published by Moondream Press (an imprint of Copper Dog Publishing LLC).

He has written three collections of poetry: *Autumn Blush* and *Jubilant Whispers* whose second editions will soon be published by Racket River Press (an imprint of Copper Dog Publishing LLC), and *Dark Parchments.*

In the upcoming year Michael will not only be overseeing the writing of the new Sha'Daa anthology *Sha'Daa: Inked,* but he is also overseeing the writing of the shared-world novel *Not To Yield,* a science fiction tale inspired by The Odyssey.

Michael is the Founder of the international writers club, *The Fictioneers,* a non-profit organization created in 2007 to encourage the writing of sci fi, fantasy, and horror, and the creative interaction of fledgling writers with more experienced professionals. *The Fictioneers* is loosely modeled after those fun children's clubs of mid-20th Century radio fame (Captain Midnight, Little Orphan Annie, etc.).

All of the illustrations in *Dark Parchments* are historical works in the public domain.

Copper Dog Publishing LLC

OUR IMPRINTS

SCIENCE FICTION, HORROR AND FANTASY

POETRY

Pumpkin Hill Press

CHILDRENS' TITLES

To find out more about our imprints
and our upcoming releases, visit our website:
www.CopperDogPublishing.com
or our Facebook page:
www.facebook.com/copperdogpublishing